We're Off to Harvard Square...

ISBN 1-889833-86-X

Cover and interior design
by Laura McFadden
laura.mcfadden@rcn.com

Printed in Canada.

Published by Commonwealth Editions
an imprint of Memoirs Unlimited, Inc.
266 Cabot Street, Beverly, Massachusetts 01915
www.commonwealtheditions.com

We're Off to Harvard Square...

Commonwealth Editions
Beverly, Massachusetts

Rickety brick,

   Rickety brick,

      We're off to Harvard Square . . .

See jumbles and heaps . . .

Hear **rumbles**

and **beeps** . . .

And **chat** by the chess-player's **chair**.

Skedaddle

down

Brattle...

See rowers with paddles...

And **bookbags**
and **backpacks**
galore.

Regroup at the Coop

out in front by the stoop

to munch lunch at a neighboring store.

Want **pizza**?

Or pancakes?

Pulled pork or pot pie?

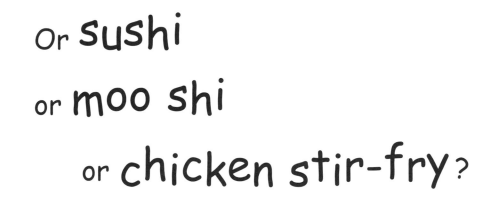

Or sushi
or moo shi
or chicken stir-fry?

Italian with scallion

or

Russian-baked blintz

With savory saffron

and marvelous mints.

Then it's time for our ice cream...

Piled **high** up in cones . . .

Dumped deep down in dishes . .

Or **wrapped** right in scones!

Mashed up with moosh-ins...

Or drizzled with drip...

Let's **veto** vanilla...

For **chocolate-chunk chip!**

When we're **full** and we're **tired**,

there's just one place to be—

At a curbside café

for a **calm** cup of tea.

There we'll sip steaming mugs

while surveying the Square . . .

See the **man** with the **mohawk**,

The **girl** with **green** hair.

The students **stock up** at the store **discount** bin.

A magician-man balances bars on his chin.

Then the **daylight** grows **dusky**,

The **stars** all **aglow** . . .

The **evening** musicians

come put on their **shows**.

So to sweet strains of singing

and twinkling lights,

Let's pack up our things

and bid Cambridge goodnight.

Meg Birnbaum

Sage Stossel is a native of Belmont, Massachusetts, and a graduate of Harvard College (1993), where she contributed a weekly cartoon strip, "Jody," to the *Harvard Crimson*. She is an editor at *The Atlantic Monthly* and the books editor of *The Radcliffe Quarterly*. Her editorial cartoon feature, "Sage, Ink," appears regularly in *The Atlantic Monthly Online*. She lives in Cambridge, Massachusetts.